USBORNE TRUE STORIES

ESCAPE

USBORNE TRUE STORIES

ESCAPE

by Paul Dowswell

Reading consultant: Alison Kelly
Edited by Jane Chisholm and Rachel Firth
Designed by Sarah Cronin
Cover designed by Matthew Preston
Cover illustration by Adrian Stone
Inside illustrations by Ian McNee

First published in 2018 by Usborne Publishing Ltd., Usborne House,
83-85 Saffron Hill, London EC1N 8RT, England.
www.usborne.com

A CIP catalogue record for this book is available from the British Library.

CONTENTS

CHAPTER ONE

BREAKOUT AT ALCATRAZ

Frank Morris breathed in the salty sea air and shivered in the sharp January sunshine. Peering over the wall of the exercise yard, he could see city streets a mile and a half away over the freezing waters of San Francisco Bay. Sometimes, when the wind was blowing in the right direction, you could even hear the traffic. But here he was, in the midwinter of 1960, stuck in Alcatraz high security prison on the first day of a twelve year sentence.

In the 1930s, Morris reflected, Alcatraz had

been one of the most notorious prisons in the world. Known as 'The Rock', people had said it was escape proof and, so far, they had been right. They used to put America's most notorious prisoners in there – 'Creepy' Karpis, 'Machine Gun' Kelly, Al Capone… but not any more. The villains were no longer notorious, although they were often just as brutal. Now the island was a dumping ground for troublesome prisoners like him, a bank robber and burglar, who'd managed to escape from every prison they'd put him in. He refused to accept that 'The Rock' was an exception. Although no one else had managed it, from the moment he arrived on the island, he was planning his getaway.

Morris was a gaunt, handsome man, not unlike Clint Eastwood, who would later play him in a Hollywood movie. His pleasant face and quiet, amiable manner disguised a ruthless determination and razor-sharp mind. As his first days at Alcatraz went by, Morris got used to the prison routine. There was the daily visit to the workshop to earn money, making brushes or gloves. There were the routine body searches, half-hourly head counts, the two hours of 'recreation' wandering around the exercise yard. Then there were the three meals a day in the prison canteen. The canteen was considered to be one of the most dangerous places in the prison. As a precaution against an outbreak of rioting, rifle slits had been built into the walls, and silver tear-gas bombs nestled in the ceiling.

After the evening meal, the prisoners were locked in their cells for the night. They had four hours to themselves before lights out at 9:00pm. Here they could paint, read, play musical instruments, all in the relative privacy of their cells. Some called out chess moves to opponents nearby; others swapped jibes and threats with prisoners they planned to attack during an afternoon exercise period.

Morris's easy manner soon made him friends. In the cell next to him was Allen West, an accordion-playing New York car thief. The two men got along well. In the canteen, where the prisoners could sit where they liked at meal times on long tables and benches, Morris also met the Anglin brothers, John and Clarence. They were burly country boys, who'd left behind a life as Florida farmhands for a career in bank robbery, and now they were prison veterans. They had cells on the same row as Morris and West, but further down the row.

A whole year went by before Morris discovered something he could really use to help him escape. Another prisoner told him that a large fan motor had been removed from a rooftop ventilator shaft three years before. It had never been replaced. Morris's sharp mind instantly pictured a daring nocturnal getaway through the shaft. There was a way out of 'The Rock' thirty feet above his head. An escape would be difficult but not impossible. One thing was certain – it would take a great deal of time and planning. But time is the only luxury a man has during his term of imprisonment, and Morris was going to make the most of it.

The first thing Morris had to do was to figure out a way of getting from a locked cell up to the roof. The men were watched closely during the time they were let out of their cells, so going up there then would be impossible. Then one day, inspiration struck. At the bottom of every cell, just below the sink, sat a small air vent. Behind it lay a narrow corridor carrying water, electricity and sewer pipes. If Morris could remove the vent and then make a hole big enough for him to crawl through, he would be able to climb up to the ventilator shaft and out on to the roof. At night he was left alone in his cell for a whole nine hours. This would be a perfect time to explore.

But how easy would it be to make that hole? Morris stooped down and picked at the concrete around the vent with a pair of steel nail clippers. Tiny flakes fell away. The concrete could be dug out but it would take ages to do it. And making the hole wasn't the only problem. Hiding it as it got bigger was also a major consideration.

Morris decided he could order an accordion, like West's, to hide his early excavations, paying for it with money he'd earned from the prison workshop. As the hole grew slowly bigger and became too big to conceal with the accordion, Morris hit on the idea of making a false wall with a painted board, complete with a painted-on air vent.

The more Morris plotted, the more he realized an escape like this would be better made with others to help him. West and the Anglin brothers were quickly recruited. Their closeness to him in the cell block would help. The four became an escape committee, and their first move was for them all to take up painting as a hobby. This gave them a seemingly innocent excuse to order brushes, paints and drawing boards, which they could each use to make a false wall when it was needed.

While West watched out for patrolling guards from his cell next door, Morris began to chip away at the concrete with his clippers. After a slow hour he had collected a small pile of fragments, and his fingers ached terribly.

He grumbled quietly to West: "I reckon at this rate we'll still be digging by the time we come up for parole."

"We'll have to have ourselves a little talk with the Anglins at breakfast," said West, and the two retired to their bunks to sleep.

"Well…"

Clarence Anglin always left a word hanging in the air, but what he went on to say was almost always worth waiting for. West and Morris listened intently.

"See this spoon? I reckon we can make ourselves a proper digging tool with this. You stick your clippers to that handle, and you get a lot more digging done."

Morris slipped his spoon into his pocket.

"Great idea, Clarence," he said. "And I know just how to put spoon and blade together! Catch you later…"

That night, as other men painted, or played their instruments, Morris prepared his cell for some ingenious improvised metalwork. First he broke the handle off his stolen spoon, and then removed one of the blades from his nail clippers.

"Hey Westy," he whispered, "You got a dime?"

"Yeah, who's asking?"

"Gimme it, I'll pay you back when we break out of here! Now keep a lookout for me."

Morris began to chip off tiny slivers of silver from the dime until he had made a little pile on his table. Then he tied fifty or so matches into a tight bundle. Next he piled some books into two close towers and positioned the spoon handle and clipper blade in the gap between the books so that they were touching. Finally he carefully sprinkled the silver slivers on top of the spoon and blade.

"Anyone coming? Good. Here goes!"

WHOOOOOOOSH. Morris ignited the bundle of matches beneath the handle and blade and, for a brief second or two, they were bathed in a fierce white heat, which quickly settled into a fast burning orange flame.

"Bingo!" he cried quietly to himself. Sure enough, the heat had melted the silver, and fused the handle and blade together.

"What's that smell, Frank? You raising the devil in there?" said West, who caught a strong whiff of burning matches.

Morris checked to see that no guard was approaching, then quickly passed his new tool through the bars and into West's cell.

"No kidding," said West. "I'm gonna get me one of these!"

Soon, all four men had made themselves similar digging tools. But hacking away at the concrete was still hard, tedious work. After all, the wall was eight inches thick.

"There's got to be a better way than this," thought Morris, and sure enough, there was.

Allen West enjoyed his job as a prison cleaner. He could wander around chatting with people, and still appear to be working at the same time. The job also brought him several unexpected perks, such as access to electrical equipment.

"What we need is the inside of a vacuum cleaner, and I know just where to find one," he said to Morris. "Take the motor out for the fan, stick in a drill bit on that pivot that goes around, and what have you got – a power drill!!"

"You get me a vacuum motor, and I'll get you a drill bit," said Morris.

West smuggled a motor into his cell, and Morris fitted it up with a drill bit he had stolen from the prison workshop. They both knew it would be terribly noisy so they had to wait until the prison music hour – when the men were allowed to play their instruments in the cells – before they could try it out.

Morris placed the motor's plug into the light socket in his cell.

"Well, here goes…"

He flicked the switch and the motor whirred

into life. That was loud enough, but the noise it made when the bit hit the concrete was excruciating. Morris drilled for as long as he dared and then stopped. The results were promising. Two holes had gone right through to the other side. Working around these with the blade would be a lot quicker.

Next morning at breakfast, Morris told the Anglins how things had gone.

"We'll pass this drill around between the four of us, but we need to use it real careful," he said. "Just make a series of holes when you can, when everyone's blowing, scraping, strumming and honking. This is gonna save us months of digging. Once we got the holes in the wall, digging the rest out with the blades at night will be a walk in the park."

Clarence's eyes lit up. His fingers were completely covered with blisters.

With the escape now looking increasingly likely, the men turned their thoughts to getting off the island. Sitting together at the evening meal, they pondered the problems that faced them.

"Water's freezing cold. You got fog almost all year round. Wouldn't like to go to all the trouble of escaping just to freeze to death in that water," said Clarence between mouthfuls.

"The swim's been done," said West. "I heard three girls did it back in '33."

Morris was more realistic: "But they were athletes. They trained for months. They probably covered themselves with goose grease to keep warm, and they definitely weren't living on no prison diet to strengthen them up for the swim… and I'll bet they had a support boat follow them over. What we need is a little assistance: a raft, life jacket, something to keep us afloat, or even better, out of that water."

John Anglin spoke next. "I seen a whole pile of plastic raincoats just lying by the workshop. We could steal some of them, take the sleeves off and blow them up like water wings. We could even stick them on any stray planks by the water's edge and make ourselves a raft."

Morris smiled broadly. "As soon as we've got behind that wall, we can start collecting things."

The holes in the wall were getting bigger every day, so the four hurried to complete the false walls that would cover up their handiwork. They painted drawing boards the same shade as the cell wall, and then painted on an air vent. Then they carefully chipped away the wall just around the vent, so that their false wall would fit over it without jutting out.

In bright light the fake walls wouldn't survive a second look, but in the dim recess of a cell they blended in well enough. Now they could dig with less fear of discovery, and soon they had made holes which were big enough to squeeze through.

Getting out at night presented a major problem though. All the doors on the cells at Alcatraz were made of steel bars – this meant a patrolling guard could look into any cells at any time of day or night to check on the convict inside. But Morris had come up with what he thought was a brilliant solution. Torn pages from magazines were soaked in his cell sink. Then the soggy paper was mashed into a pulp to make papier-mâché, and fashioned into the shape of a head.

After a week or so, the head was dry enough to paint. Clarence Anglin, who worked as a prison barber, smuggled Morris some hair the same shade as his, which added a final authentic touch. Morris used the hair to add eyebrows too. Poking out of a blanket at the top of a bunk, in a darkened cell the head would look just like a real one. Rolled-up bedding and clothes would make a body shape under the blankets. The prototype head completed, Allen and the Anglins set about making their own dummy heads.

Finally, the night had come to take a trip to the roof. Morris spent the day beforehand trying to curb his restlessness. What if the way up to the roof was blocked? What if the ventilator motor had been replaced after all? All their painstaking work would be wasted. The 12-year sentence stretched out before him. Then another awful thought occurred. The holes in the wall would be discovered eventually, and that would mean he would have to serve even longer.

At last, night fell, and activity in the prison slowly ground to a halt. As West kept an eye out for the guard, Morris placed the dummy head on his pillow and wriggled through the hole at the back of his cell, carefully replacing the false wall behind him.

The corridor behind the wall was a grim, damp place, which stank of the seawater that flowed through its sewage pipes. All around him were ducts and cables, and dust and dirt had settled on everything he touched. Even so, standing up in the tiny corridor Morris felt a huge gleeful rush, like a naughty boy doing something a hated teacher had expressly forbidden.

He had to wait a while for his eyes to become accustomed to the gloom, then he began to make his way up, climbing through a tangle of conduits, mesh, wiring and catwalks to reach the roof ventilator shaft. It stood before him, hanging down five feet from the roof.

The first thing he realized was that he would need someone else to help lift him inside, and he congratulated himself on having asked the others to join his escape plan. Morris also noted that there was plenty of space up there. In this rarely visited and unguarded area of the prison, it would be a perfect place to store material for their long swim to the mainland, a mile or so away.

The next night, Morris and Clarence Anglin made a trip to the roof together. Clarence lifted him inside, but what Morris saw there came like a punch to the stomach. The fan blade and motor had been removed all right, but they had been replaced by two iron bars, a grille and a rainhood, all firmly anchored in place by solid steel rivets.

They shared the news next morning with West.

"What did you expect to find?" he chided.

"A couple of airline tickets to Brazil? We got through eight inches of that concrete, so a few bolts ain't gonna stop us now."

West was right. Morris chewed over the problem for a couple of days and came up with a solution. The two bars could be bent back with a length of pipe a repairman had carelessly left in the back corridor. The rivets that held the grille and rainhood in place were more of a problem. The vacuum cleaner drill would have been handy, but it would make far too much noise. What they needed was something to cut through the rivets. The workshop had a supply of carborundum string – a thin cord coated with abrasive powder, used to saw through metal. Using that would take many more hours of painstaking work, but it could be done.

So, most nights, a couple of the escapers would climb up to the roof and saw and saw. It was tedious, painful work, but eventually the rivets came away. Morris thought up the clever idea of replacing them with rivet-shaped balls of soap, which they painted black. He didn't want a patrolling guard to peer into the shaft and notice the rivets were missing.

By now, it was midsummer, 1962. Everything was in place, and there would be no better time of year for an escape. The coldness of the water around the prison made it lethal at most other times. Hunched together in the canteen, they haggled about when they should go.

"I say now, and John's with me," said Clarence Anglin. "We've got a huge pile of raincoats waiting to be discovered up in the roof, and those holes in our cells ain't gonna stay secret forever."

"True enough," said West. "My fake wall keeps slipping too when I'm outta there at night. I'm gonna have to fix it in with cement, so let's set a date that will give me time to chip it all out again."

"We'll go in ten or so days," said Morris. "I'm gonna pay a visit to the library, and get me a book on tides. Water in the Bay's dangerous, so we've got to go at a good time, otherwise we'll end up dead."

But over the next week, things were getting even more worrying. Convicts would return to their cells after mealtimes and notice small differences – a towel moved here, a book moved there – that gave away the fact that their cell had been searched. Perhaps it was just routine checks, or perhaps the prison guards suspected that an escape was coming.

Three days after their last conversation with West, the Anglins could wait no longer. About 9:00pm on the evening of June 11th, Morris heard a voice behind his wall. It was John Anglin telling him that he and Clarence were going NOW. Before Morris could argue, John had headed back up the corridor. Next door, West was panic-stricken. Unprepared, and choking with anger and frustration, he began chipping at the hardened cement seal he had placed around his fake wall.

Morris kept watch for him as long as he could. It was just before lights-out, and the prisoners had yet to settle down for the night. For now, the dull bustle of conversation and activity drowned out West's frantic digging, but Morris could not stay watching out for him much longer.

When the lights were turned off for the night, Morris had to go. He left West digging away, and headed up to the roof. The Anglins were already up there waiting for him. There was no point arguing with them about what they had done to West. They just had to get on and see the escape through without him.

John lifted Morris up to the shaft and quickly removed the soap rivet heads, his face starkly lit by the flash of the lighthouse beacon as it swept over the roof. Morris gently eased the grille from its moorings and onto the floor of the roof. But as he lifted away the rainhood, it caught in a sudden gust of wind, and clattered noisily to the floor. Inside the vent, Morris froze. He was so tense he could hardly move.

The three men waited, stock-still in the dark,

expecting to hear alarm bells or shouts, and guards rushing up to investigate. Down below, a patrolling guard had indeed heard the noise, and hurried off to tell the duty officer.

"Don't worry about it," he was told. "There's lots of garbage on the roof. It's probably an old paint can blowing around in the wind."

Ten minutes passed before they thought it would be safe to move. Each man slowly slithered out onto the roof, with three or four raincoat sleeves tucked around his belt. They all blinked in the harsh glare of the lighthouse beacon. Away from the stuffy hothouse of the prison, the night air felt cool, and the salty sea breeze caught in their nostrils.

The route from rooftop to shore passed through brightly floodlit areas, overlooked by gun towers. There was a lot to do before they could get safely away. They hugged the shadows as best they could and crawled to the edge of the roof. Morris hauled himself over the rim of the roof and onto a pipe.

Below was a fifty foot drop. He moved with infinite slowness, in case any sudden movement should catch the eye of a guntower guard. He slid down the pipe with the same slow care, and waited for the Anglins to follow.

Away from the cell block the three men carefully made their way over a couple of fences and down a shallow cliff to the seashore. Across the water, the mainland beckoned, just a mile and a half away. Crouching in the damp sand, and shivering in the sharp sea breeze, they blew into their raincoat water wings, then waded into the freezing waters of San Francisco Bay…

West finally chipped away his false wall after midnight. He hurried up to the roof, but Morris and the Anglins were long gone. Poking his head through the ventilator he disturbed a flock of seagulls. They made such a screeching he fled back to his cell in panic. He spent the rest of his sentence wondering what would have happened if the Anglins had given him fair warning of the escape. Maybe he'd be in a quiet backwater bar, with a long cool drink and a beautiful girl. Maybe he'd be lying at the bottom of San Francisco Bay, his bleached bones picked clean by crabs.

AFTER THE ESCAPE

At daybreak, guards sent to rouse the missing men found only dummy heads in their empty beds. Other prison officers recalled the noise that roused their suspicions the night before, and estimated that the men must have entered the water at around ten o'clock that evening. It was a good time to go. The Bay was calm, the currents were just right. If the escapers had survived the cold, they had every chance of reaching the mainland.

Boats, soldiers and guards with dogs were all sent out to find them. After two days, all they had turned up was a plastic bag full of family photographs belonging to Clarence Anglin.

After that, nothing. No bodies. No clothing.

No sightings. The three could have been washed out to sea and drowned, but it is equally likely they escaped. They may even still be alive today, although they would all be very old men.

The getaway from 'escape proof' Alcatraz soon became national news, and a severe embarrassment to the prison authorities. The chief guard, Olin Blackwell, had to admit that the concrete structure of the prison was crumbling away, and that this had allowed the prisoners to dig out from their cells.

At the time of the escape, many government officials felt that the prison had outlived its usefulness. So, in 1963, all the inmates were shipped off the island and dispersed throughout the American prison system.

In 1979, Clint Eastwood starred as Frank Morris in the movie *Escape from Alcatraz*, which was made mostly on the island. The movie production company spent $500,000 reconnecting electricity and redecorating the prison, which had been closed for 16 years. Most of the actors working on the movie became ill in the musty interior of the prison, which gave their performances a realistic convict lethargy. The movie brought the escape of Morris and the Anglins to a global audience, and today Alcatraz is a popular tourist attraction.

Relatives of the Anglins say they have received postcards from South America from the brothers, but have never produced them to prove this. Morris, who had no close family, has vanished without trace. Allen West was released from prison in 1967 but was back behind bars the following year. He died in a Florida prison in 1978.

CHAPTER TWO

ALIAS IVAN BAGEROV

"Getting out of here is going to be a piece of cake. It's getting away that's going to be difficult."

British Royal Navy Lieutenant David James was explaining his escape plan to a fellow prisoner, Captain David Wells. It was early winter in 1943, four years into the Second World War. James had concocted two ingenious disguises for himself, to get him from the prison camp to nearby Sweden, from where he would be able to return to Britain.

The two men were sitting in front of a coal fire

32

in their sparsely-furnished hut at Marlag und Milag Nord Prisoner of War Camp, near Bremen, Germany. Outside the window, a dreary, freezing rain had been falling all day. The north German winter had settled in with a vengeance.

James outlined his escape in more detail.

"This is how I see it… I'm a foreigner who speaks only a few words of German. So, I'm going to disguise myself as another foreigner. The guards and officials I'm going to meet will see scores of passes and identity papers every day. They'll know them like the back of their hand, and will be able to spot a fake from 20 paces. So, I'm going for something unusual they won't have seen before. In fact, I'm going as a Bulgarian!"

Wells looked puzzled.

"Why?"

James went on, "As you know, the Bulgarians are Germany's allies, but no one here knows much about them. They wouldn't know a Bulgarian if one came up and punched them on the nose. Also,

I thought, if I adapt my own navy uniform to look as if I might be in the Bulgarian Navy, then no one will know what that looks like either. I certainly don't."

Wells laughed.

"Bulgarian Navy! They've only got about three ships. You're on a winning streak there, old chap. What have you got?"

James showed him his props. A friend in the camp, who had been a tailor before the war, had made him a gold and blue shoulder insignia with the letters KBVMF, which stood for Royal Bulgarian Navy.

"Those letters look strange. They're Russian, aren't they?" said Wells.

"Yes," said James. "They use the same alphabet as the Russians. In fact, that's part of the next step in my plan. I've had a whole bunch of documents forged by a chap over in Hut D. He used to work as a book illustrator, and he's done a brilliant job. Look at this!"

James went to his locker and took out a folder full of papers, letters, passes and a big photograph.

"Here's my identity card. Lieutenant Ivan Bagerov – Royal Bulgarian Navy. All that Bulgarian writing won't mean a thing to your average guard."

Wells laughed.

"Who's that handsome chap in the identity card photo? It's certainly not YOU!"

James smiled.

"We found him in a German magazine. He's a German Navy hero. Looks a bit like me, but we put that fake Bulgarian stamp over half his face, so it wouldn't be too obvious it isn't! I've made sure everything in my case looks as if it could be Bulgarian. I even scraped the manufacturer's stamp off my English soap and etched in a Bulgarian letter."

"Who's that in the big photo?" said Wells. "It looks like that famous ballet dancer. What's her name?"

James laughed again.

"That is Margot Fonteyn. Lovely, isn't she! I'm going to tell anyone searching my case that she's my Bulgarian fiancée. It should prove to be quite a nice distraction. You know Roberts over in Hut E? He speaks Russian, so I got him to write me a love letter too. We're covering all the angles here! And I've even changed the English labels on my clothes. I couldn't get Bulgarian or Russian labels, but a couple of Greek fellows in the camp have given me some of theirs. They look different. And, on top of everything, Bulgaria is also a monarchy, so the crown on my Royal Navy jacket buttons won't look out of place either. And then there's THIS!"

James took out another forged document.

"It's a letter of introduction from The Royal Bulgarian Navy. It's written in German and I'm going to show it to anyone who bothers me, or who I think could help me. It says: 'Lieutenant Bagerov is engaged in liaison duties of a technical nature which involve him in much travel. Since he speaks very little German, the usual kind assistance of all German officials is confidently requested on his behalf.'

Wells laughed at the daring plan. He was certainly impressed. But then he looked worried.

"Uh-oh," he said. "I'm not sure it will work, James. Quite a few of our Navy chaps here have been into Bremen over the last few weeks to visit the hospital. Your Navy uniform might be a bit different, but it's not different enough. I'm sure someone will recognize it and have you nabbed."

"I've thought of that too. I'm going to start my escape in another disguise! I've got some silk patches to put over the brass buttons of my jacket, and a cloth cap made from a jacket lining, and a scarf and a pair of old canvas trousers. I'm going to become Christof Lindholm – Danish electrician! I've got a pass for that too."

"Crikey, you've been busy!" said Wells. "So what happens when you get to Sweden, or even Britain, and you need to prove who you really are?"

"I've got that sorted out too. I've sewn my real

identity papers into my jacket lining, so I can go back to being me when I need to."

"Well, best of luck – though with all that lot I don't think you'll need it," said Wells.

James looked a little ill at ease.

"Frankly, old chap, sitting in front of this lovely fire, with the rain coming down outside, I'm not sure I want to escape at all. But so many people have helped me with this scheme I feel I've got to give it a go."

James's friends at the camp gave him all the German money they could spare and then he was ready to go. On the morning of December 8th, 1943, he made his way down to the shower block on the edge of the camp. Amazingly, a window there opened onto the street outside. All James had to do was to change into his Danish electrician's outfit, and squeeze out when he was sure no one was coming.

Walking away in his disguise, he could have been any local workman. But trouble loomed almost as soon as he left the camp. He was stopped by a policeman who immediately became suspicious. James began to panic. All that work and here he was, barely a minute away from the camp, and about to be caught red-handed. The policeman looked in his case. Fortunately it just contained some clothes. James had carefully hidden all Ivan Bagerov's documents – they were strapped to his leg with adhesive bandages.

The policeman began to question him in a hostile way. What was he doing? Who was he? Who was he staying with? It was a nightmare moment. James only spoke a few words of German, but blurted out that he was staying with the local priest. He didn't even know his name, so just referred to him as 'Father'.

The policeman was still suspicious. What did the priest look like? James made a wild guess. He was an old man with silver hair, he said, which fortunately turned out to be true. He stumbled on with more of his story, hoping that the policeman didn't start to wonder why this supposed Danish workman had such an odd accent.

The story wasn't working. The policeman told him to come with him to the police station. But James had another trick up his sleeve – a forged letter from a local hospital, telling him to report there that afternoon. This final detail convinced the policeman that James was the Danish electrician he was pretending to be. The man dismissed him with a curt "Good day" and James hurried off, feeling quite sick and doing his best to stop his legs from trembling as he walked.

He reached Bremen station without further trouble, and headed at once to the public toilet. There, the cap and canvas trousers of his electrician's outfit were hidden behind a cistern. Away from the middle of the town, James felt it was now safe to take on his Bulgarian disguise. Inside the tiny toilet cubicle, he removed the silk patches from his buttons, sewed on the shoulder insignia, and darkened his light hair with theatrical make-up, to make him look more Eastern European.

Christof Lindholm had disappeared – and out stepped Ivan Bagerov. Taking a deep breath to steady his nerves, James walked up to a station guard, and presented him with his forged letter of introduction.

The man read the letter and gave James a smile.

"Where are you going to, sir?" he said.

James told him he was heading for the port of Lübeck, on the Baltic Sea. This would be the perfect spot to head for Sweden.

"Follow me, sir," said the guard briskly, and they walked off to the ticket office.

James's letter worked like a charm. The guard found out which trains he would have to take, wrote down the details for him, and gave him a ticket. Then he took him to the station waiting room and bought him a beer from the bar! James had to struggle to stop himself from laughing out loud, or gushing with gratitude. He wanted to give the man a big hug, but forced himself to remain calm.

The train arrived, and James was soon heading for the coast. The officials he met on his way – ticket inspectors, policemen, guards – all stared blankly at his Bulgarian pass, and waved him on his way with a polite nod.

After a couple of hours the train pulled into Hamburg, where James needed to change trains. He had to spend an hour in the waiting room, and here he was stared at suspiciously by a German soldier. James was sure this man had seen through his disguise and recognized his Royal Navy uniform, but he decided to bluff it out. He thought "What would I do if I was really Ivan Bagerov and someone was staring at me? Why, stare straight back!"

James glared at the man with such hostility the soldier became embarrassed and let his gaze slip to the floor. He left the waiting room shortly afterwards. James wondered if he had gone to fetch a policeman, but by the time the train arrived no one had come to bother him.

The journey passed slowly. James had to get off the train again to spend an uncomfortable night in a waiting room in Bad Kleinen, but he had covered two hundred miles in a single day. His escape was going better than he could ever have imagined.

The next day the train continued on to Stettin, another port on the Baltic Sea. James thought he would try his luck here, as Stettin was just as likely to have Swedish ships as Lübeck.

But it didn't. As James wandered along the waterfront there was not a single Swedish ship to be seen. Cursing his luck, he headed into the town, and went to several bars, hoping to overhear some Swedish voices.

By late afternoon James realized Stettin had been a big mistake. There was nothing else to do but continue on his journey. So he returned to the station and caught a train heading to Lübeck. Again, he had to get off the train in the evening, and spent another uncomfortable night in the dining room of a very crowded military rest camp. As James tried to sleep at a table in the corner of the room, he was joined by several German naval officers. He couldn't have wished for worse company. He felt sure they would recognize his British uniform, but they must have been even more tired than he was, for they said nothing and didn't even give him a second glance.

Next day he hurried off to the station and arrived in Lübeck by late morning. By now his smart lieutenant image was beginning to look a bit shabby, especially as he had two days of stubble on his chin. James headed for the nearest barber and asked, in halting German, if he could have a shave. The barber looked at him in astonishment.

"Don't you know?" the man said rather rudely. "Don't you know about the soap ration? No one has had a shave at a barbers for two years!"

James gave an embarrassed shrug, and fled from the shop in a near panic, certain that everyone in the street was looking at him.

Feeling flustered, he booked himself into a hotel, where he left his suitcase, and headed for the docks. The first thing he saw on the quayside were two Swedish ships. But between him and them were guarded dock gates.

A guard stood at one side of the road, so James followed a large truck which was going into the docks, taking care that he stayed on the other side of it from the guard. Once on the quayside he walked up the gangplank of the nearest Swedish ship, and headed for the crew quarters. The ship was taking on a cargo of coal, and coal dust hung in the chilly winter air, making him cough.

James could hear Swedish voices coming from a cabin, and knocked on the steel door. He walked in and saw two men sitting at a table sipping coffee. They looked up expectantly. Then one of them smiled and spoke to him in excellent English.

"Royal Navy, I believe. I'd recognize your

uniform a mile away!"

James laughed. He was relieved that the man was so friendly.

"Yes," said James. "It's not much of a disguise. I'm actually supposed to be Ivan Bagerov of the Royal Bulgarian Navy!"

The men invited James to share a cup of coffee with them, and he told them his story, and asked if they would take him to Sweden.

The man who spoke English gave a sorry shrug.

"Look my friend, I'd love to help, but it can't be done. When this coal is loaded into the hold, we've got several German dockhands coming on board to refuel the ship. They're bound to see you on board, and if they suspect you're a stowaway, then we'll all be arrested. You can see for yourself that the ship's just too small for there to be anywhere to hide you."

James was crestfallen. The man had been so friendly he felt sure he would help him. He had even begun to think his ordeal was almost over.

"Please," he begged. "I've been on the run for three days now, and this is the first time I've felt safe. There must be somewhere I can hide?"

But the Swede had made up his mind. He spoke firmly, in a tone that made it plain that there was nothing more to discuss.

"I'd like to help you, but I certainly don't want to end up in a concentration camp. Look over there," he said, pointing out of the cabin porthole. "That ship is heading for Sweden, too. It's leaving any minute, so try your luck there."

That was that. James thanked the man and got up to leave. Standing on the deck, he surveyed the route down the gangplank and onto the other ship. Having felt so safe and near to success mere minutes ago, the trip between this ship and the next seemed terribly dangerous. James's nerve was finally going.

As he walked down the plank, he saw to his horror that the other ship was about to leave the quayside. James ran, but he was too late.

For one crazy moment he thought he could just leap on board, but he was sure he would be spotted and the boat would be stopped before it left German waters.

"Right," he said to himself, "back to the hotel, to try again tomorrow." But now, dispirited and exhausted, James became careless. He did not bother to hide from the guard at the entrance of the dock, and he was spotted and stopped. Perhaps his unshaven appearance gave him away, for this time the Ivan Bagerov story didn't work. The guard insisted that James go with him to the local police station to have his papers checked more thoroughly.

There was nothing James could do but go. Besides, there was still a chance that the police would be as baffled as everyone else had been by his Bulgarian documents.

Shortly afterwards, James stood in front of the desk of a senior officer at Lübeck police station. The man examined his identity card with a magnifying glass and said, quite casually, in English:

"So, where did you escape from?"

James, who had been holding his breath in anticipation, let out a long sigh. Actually, he felt quite relieved that it was all over.

The policeman was surprisingly polite. He offered James a seat and called in several of his colleagues. One of them mocked the forged pass, but another congratulated James on such a good forgery. Everyone seemed quite amused by his tale, which made James feel more at ease. After all, he had heard that escapers were sometimes shot if they were caught. The man who escorted him back to the local military jail even told him he was sorry he had had such bad luck.

James was sent back to Marlag und Milag Nord and spent ten days in solitary confinement in a punishment cell. His desire to escape had not left him. Five weeks later he was gone again, this time disguised as a merchant seaman. Taking the same route, he successfully boarded a ship to Sweden.

This time he got there, and was able to make his way safely back to England.

AFTER THE ESCAPE

Once home, James wrote *An Escaper's Progress*, an account of his adventures in Marlag und Milag Nord. He noted that being an escaper is like meeting someone at a party whose name you cannot remember. You have to pick up clues as you talk, by asking leading questions, all to make your disguise more convincing. In this way he learned how to get by without drawing attention to himself in the places and situations he found himself in.

After the war, James became an Antarctic explorer, and was a Conservative Member of Parliament. He also helped to set up the Loch Ness Investigation Bureau, an organization dedicated to finding evidence of the Loch Ness Monster. He died in 1986.

CHAPTER THREE

A SPY IN THE SCRUBS

Night fell early on Saturday October 22nd, 1966. An overcast sky and chill north wind reminded visitors to London's Hammersmith Hospital that winter was coming. By the side of the hospital was a small alleyway, which separated it from Wormwood Scrubs prison. Parked in the alley, in a nondescript blue car, sat an anxious-looking man, cradling a bunch of chrysanthemums.

Anybody who noticed him would think he was planning to visit a relative in the hospital. But if they looked at him for longer than a couple of seconds they would see he was talking to his chrysanthemums in a rather agitated way. The man was Sean Bourke, and what he was actually doing was speaking into a walkie-talkie radio hidden in the flowers. He was about to commit an exceptionally serious crime.

Wormwood Scrubs, a dreary Victorian building, was home to many of London's small-time criminals. Most had been given short sentences, and none were considered particularly dangerous, apart from one. Among the burglars, car thieves and sellers of stolen goods, was an infamous spy. His name was George Blake and he was a former senior officer in the British secret service. Blake had betrayed at least 42 British agents to Soviet Russia, and passed on other vital top secret information to Britain's enemies.

His trial in 1961 had caused a sensation. He had been sentenced to 42 years in prison, the longest term ever given to a spy in peacetime. Blake had been sent to Wormwood Scrubs, in West London, because the British secret service wanted to talk to him from time to time. Their offices were in London, so it was convenient to have him nearby. With hindsight this was not a smart move. A high security prison would have been more appropriate for such a clever man.

Blake had a fascinating, tangled history. Born Georg Behar in Holland, of a Dutch mother and Jewish father, his loyalty lay with his political beliefs, rather than any one country. He fought with the Dutch resistance when the country was taken over by the Nazis in 1940, then escaped to Britain in 1943. He joined the Royal Navy, where he was recruited into the British secret service.

Caught up in the Korean War, Blake survived three years as a prisoner of the North Koreans. On his return, he had become convinced communism was the best system of government, and gave top secret information to the Soviet Union, the world's leading communist nation, for almost ten years.

Curiously, Blake was a popular prisoner in 'the Scrubs'. A tall, charming man, he taught illiterate prisoners to read and write, and was courteous and cooperative with the prison guards. Some prisoners sympathized with his communist views, and others felt his sentence was too harsh. He had made many friends in prison. Among them were Sean Bourke, a small-time villain, and Pat Pottle and Michael Randle – two peace activists jailed for their part in a demonstration at an American airbase in Britain. All three had recently been released from prison, and had decided to help him escape.

Now, as Bourke fidgeted outside in the gloom, Blake was standing in the bright glare of Hall D, chatting with one of the prison officers about whether television wrestling matches were faked. The guard was so engrossed in the conversation, he failed to notice another prisoner, a friend of Blake's, carefully removing two panes of glass from a large window above his head.

The conversation over, Blake headed back to

his cell, picked up a walkie-talkie radio recently smuggled into the prison, and made his way to the broken window. The hall was now virtually empty, as most guards and prisoners were at the weekly movie, which was shown every Saturday evening.

Unseen, he slipped out into the cold night air and leaped down to a porch roof below the window. From there, he jumped onto a waste container and then down to the ground. Before him stood a high brick wall.

"Sean, Sean, can you hear me?" he whispered into his walkie-talkie, as he crouched in the shadows.

But there was no reply. Bourke was busy. Two young lovers were kissing and cuddling in a car parked all too close to his own. Naturally, he didn't want any witnesses to this escape. So, pretending to be a prison official, he was busy trying to shoo the couple away.

Blake waited for what seemed like an eternity, his heart pounding in his chest and a terrible fear lurking in his stomach. The missing window panes would be spotted soon enough. Blake had been in Wormwood Scrubs for four dreary years, and the visits by the secret service men were becoming more infrequent. He knew they would soon transfer him to a more remote prison outside London, where escape would be all but impossible. This was going to be his one and only chance to get away.

Eventually Blake's radio crackled.

"George? Are you there?" said Sean Bourke. "Thank Heavens! Look, I'm throwing the ladder over now."

Another terrible, still silence followed. Then came a clattering sound as a lightweight ladder, made from washing line and knitting needles, snaked over the wall.

"OK Sean, hold tight, I'm coming over now," whispered Blake, and he ran from the shadows and out to the ladder, almost certain he would be spotted.

He climbed clumsily, scraping his fingers on the rough brickwork. Blake was not an athletic man, and this physical exercise quickly tired him. Standing on top of the wall, panting and puffing, he looked down to see Bourke and his car. Freedom was only seconds away, but Blake was so desperate to escape, he couldn't even wait that long. Rather than climbing down the outer wall, he leaped from the top, breaking a wrist and cutting his face as he landed.

"Good Heavens, man," said Bourke. "Are you all right? There was no need to do that!"

He picked up his friend and bundled him into the back of his car. Then he dashed around to the driver's seat and started the engine. The car sputtered into life, and Bourke shot off up the alley, scattering hospital visitors and crashing into the back of a car in front of him. Before the outraged driver could get out, Bourke lurched around him, and drove off to merge into the early evening traffic heading away from central London.

"We did it! We did it!" he shouted jubilantly.

In the back seat, Blake was holding his broken wrist and wincing with every bump in the road. But despite this, and the blood dripping down his face, he was grinning like a madman.

All the dull indignities of prison life flashed before him – the miserable stench of the place, the taste of limp, lukewarm cabbage, some of the Scrubs' more unpleasant residents…

"Good Lord, what I've had to put up with these last four years!" he exclaimed.

Blake was ecstatic. Then, for a second, he looked more serious.

"It's not over yet though, is it? I've got this to sort out," he said, holding up his arm, "and then I've got to get out of this country."

"All in good time, George, all in good time," said Bourke. "First we'll get you back to the hiding place I've found for you, and have something decent to eat."

It was a short journey, and as far as they could

tell no one was following them. Bourke had found Blake a room in a house, on a seedy, anonymous street not far from the prison. Bourke parked in front of the house. They waited until the street was clear, then walked in quickly before anyone spotted them.

Inside, Bourke bathed the wound on Blake's face, and bandaged up his damaged wrist as best he could. Then he left to go and dump the car a safe distance away, returning with a bottle of whisky and a bottle of brandy.

"This will help us wash down our supper," he laughed. "And wait until you see what I've got to eat!"

Bourke was soon frying two huge steaks. When they were ready, he cut Blake's into small pieces and watched as he wolfed it down with one hand. Blake was ravenously hungry, and soon had appalling indigestion.

"Four years of prison food," he laughed, "and now this. No wonder I feel sick!"

After finishing their steaks, the two men talked about the escape.

Bourke told Blake how they had planned everything, from getaway car to radio sets, knitting needle ladder to false passports.

In between drinks, they ate strawberries and cream. But while they were eating, a television show they were watching was interrupted by a news flash. The announcer declared:

"Soviet spy George Blake has escaped from Wormwood Scrubs prison, in London. The escape happened at around six thirty this evening. Blake climbed over the prison wall using a ladder thrown to him by an accomplice. The two men are believed to have driven off in a small blue car, heading west out of London."

A recent picture of Blake appeared on the screen, a prison mugshot looking stern and distant.

"A news flash!" said Bourke. "They didn't even wait for the main bulletin. You're Britain's most wanted man!"

Bourke laughed. But Blake looked more serious.

"I hope no one saw us come into the house," he said. "Every policeman in London will be looking for me."

The next day, Bourke went out to find a doctor. Blake knew that Bourke had a network of sympathetic friends, but his own background as a spy taught him that no one could really be trusted. Every contact they made like this laid them open to the possibility that someone would betray them.

Around noon, Bourke returned with a doctor, and a bundle of newspapers. The doctor was a serious young man who greeted Blake coolly, then treated his broken wrist. It was agonizing. Blake drank the last of Bourke's whisky to deaden the pain.

Bourke showed Blake the day's papers. They were full of stories of the escape. One paper had made much of the chrysanthemums Bourke had left behind in his hurry to get away. The paper painted a picture of him as a shadowy criminal mastermind, and described his chrysanthemums as a mysterious calling card.

But all this publicity was bad news. Blake's face was on the front page of every newspaper, and flashed on television at every news broadcast. They were going to have to be extremely careful.

Their first concern was the doctor who had treated Blake's wrist. To avoid the possibility of his giving them away to police, they moved to another house to stay with a man who was friends with Randle and Pottle. This move turned out to be unnecessary. The doctor never did give them away, but their new hiding place proved to be a disaster. The man's wife was being treated for mental health problems. She told her psychiatrist that they were hiding two men from the police. Another safe house was urgently needed.

Bourke too had made a silly mistake. Despite all his careful planning for the escape, he had bought the getaway car they used in his own name, and the police had traced it. Now his photograph was appearing alongside Blake's on every newspaper front page, and his name was being mentioned on every radio and television news bulletin. They now spent every day wondering when there would be a fierce knocking at the door, and they would both be whisked away to face many years in a high security prison.

In early November, they moved to Pat Pottle's house, which was also in London. Blake was now tired of all this hiding and desperate to get out of England. But, two weeks after the escape, his name and photograph were still all over the papers and television. It would be too risky to try to leave the country in the normal way, via a ferry or plane, even using a false passport.

So Pottle and Randle thought it would be a good idea to alter Blake's appearance dramatically. They gave him a drug called Meladinin which was supposed to darken his skin, and put him under a sun-lamp for several tanning sessions. The experiment was a miserable failure. Blake still

looked instantly recognizable. But Randle came
to the rescue with another ruse. This one was far
simpler.

He had a large Volkswagen camper van, and they
hid Blake in a cupboard meant for storing blankets.
Randle and his family drove to Europe, and crossed
over the border into East Germany. At the time,
this country was controlled by Soviet Russia so
Blake would be safe there.

The trip went without a hitch, and a very stiff
and slightly carsick Blake was dropped off just
outside Berlin. He introduced himself to the first
East German soldier he could find, but no one
believed his story. He was taken into the city, and a
Russian secret service officer who knew him
personally was flown over to see him. When this
officer walked in, hugged him and started to shout,
"It's him! It's him!" Blake knew his troubles
were over.

AFTER THE ESCAPE

Blake was generously rewarded by his Soviet allies. He was made a colonel in the KGB (the Soviet security service) and put up in a comfortable apartment in Moscow. He left behind a wife and three sons in England, but remarried a Russian woman and had a daughter. He found work as a researcher in international politics and economics for Moscow University. At the time of writing, Blake is still alive and in his 90s. Russian President Vladimir Putin is said to be an admirer.

CHAPTER FOUR

THE DIRTY DOCKER

If the guards at Donington Hall Prisoner of War Camp had known a bit more about Gunther Plüschow, they might have kept a closer eye on him. To the men who watched over him, he was a friendly, well-dressed fellow, who spoke very good English. He had a welcoming smile, and was good at hockey, which he played at every opportunity. He was really quite charming.

Plüschow was a prisoner of the British during the First World War. He was also extremely clever and, if he had any choice in the matter, he was not going to be staying in Donington Hall for long.

He had always done well in life. He was an excellent student at Munich's Military School, where he went age ten. He left school to join the German Imperial Army, then volunteered to become one of Germany's first air force pilots, where he rose to the rank of Captain-Lieutenant. After learning to fly, he was sent to Tsingtao in China, which was then a German colony. When the First World War broke out in 1914, Tsingtao was attacked by British and Japanese forces, and Plüschow gained a reputation as a daring flyer. While he was in China, he had had a dragon tattooed on his left arm, and his men called him 'The Dragon Master'.

The war went badly for the Germans in China and Plüschow was ordered home. On the way back, he was captured by Chinese troops, but soon escaped and took a boat from Shanghai to San Francisco. After making his way from there to New York, he took a boat to Italy. But unfortunately for him, the boat stopped at Gibraltar – a British port on the Mediterranean. Plüschow was arrested as a prisoner of war, and transported to England.

On arrival, he was sent to Donington Hall, a grand country mansion which had been turned into a prison camp. Life there was actually quite pleasant. Plüschow, who had arrived with all his luggage, was allowed to receive packages and letters from his family, and spent most of his time chatting with other German officers and playing sports.

The camp routine was very relaxed. Twice a day there was a parade for a roll call – a register to check on all the prisoners. There were different rules about how far they could go during the day, and at night. During the day they could wander through much of the grounds of the stately home, including a pleasant park, which had a high barbed wire fence around it, complete with patrolling guards. But after dark, prisoners were expected to keep to the area around their huts, known as the night boundary.

Plüschow had a good friend at the camp, another officer named Lieutenant Trefftz. Like Plüschow he spoke very good English. He also knew the country well, having visited several times. Plüschow suggested they escape together. Trefftz agreed and the two men set about planning their getaway.

Both men knew that, although getting out of the camp would be fairly easy, what came after would be the difficult part. The town of Derby was a few miles to the north of Donington. Here they planned to catch a train to London, and then hide on board a boat heading for Holland – a country that wasn't at war with either Britain or Germany.

Plüschow and Trefftz hatched a simple but ingenious escape plan based on the guards' routine. They asked their fellow prisoners to help them get away and to give them money to buy food and pay for their journey. On July 4th, 1915, the two men claimed to be ill, and the camp doctor allowed them to be excused from the daily roll call parades.

At four o'clock that afternoon, after a day resting in bed, they got up and dressed in civilian clothes. Plüschow had brought a stylish suit from China, a blue sweater and an expensive overcoat. The men were supposed to wear their uniforms at the camp, so they put their officers' caps and coats on top.

After they'd dressed, they gobbled down all the buttered rolls that had been left in the hut for the prisoners' afternoon snack. It might be several days before they ate again. Then they prepared to leave. Outside it was raining heavily. Normally they would have cursed such dismal British weather but, as Plüschow pointed out, it was perfect for their escape.

"Trefftz, my dear fellow," he said, "the gods are on our side. The guards are going to be shivering and dripping wet in their little guard boxes. They're not going to be paying much attention to us!"

"A guard box will be a better place to spend the next four hours than where we're planning to be," said Trefftz, who was not looking forward to being soaked to the skin.

The two men walked out of their hut and into the rain. Ambling rather stiffly in their many layers of clothing, they made their way over to the park. There, near the barbed wire boundary, lay a pile of deckchairs. After a quick glance around to make sure no one was watching them, the two men stooped down and hid among the chairs.

After an hour, the rain stopped, and Plüschow and Trefftz shivered and cursed in their cramped hiding place. Both were now feeling quite anxious about their escape attempt, and this tedious wait was making them jumpy.

The camp clock struck six, and the prisoners came out of their huts for the evening roll call.

"Stage one," said Plüschow. "If this fails, expect to see some bad-tempered guards with bayonets on their rifles, poking around in the undergrowth."

The two men peeked out from the chairs, as their fellow prisoners assembled. The ritual of the roll call drifted across the park, each prisoner barking a curt 'yes' as his name was called. Plüschow's and Trefftz's names were unanswered of course, but they were reported sick. As soon as the roll call was over, two of their fellow officers rushed back to occupy their beds. A camp guard was sent to check that they were there. When he saw what he thought were two sleeping figures, he assumed it was them.

Plüschow and Trefftz waited, expecting an alarm or call-out for the guards, which would tell them that their plan had failed. But everything seemed to go on as usual.

After evening roll call, the day boundary was out of bounds, and the guards withdrew to the night boundary. A slow summer dusk fell over Donington Hall, and gradually turned into a black moonless night. All Plüschow and Trefftz had to do now was climb over an unguarded barbed wire fence. But there was one more problem with the camp routine which had to be overcome. At bedtime, a guard checked every bed, but once again the escapers' fellow officers had agreed to help them. As all the prisoners were so familiar with the guards' routine, they knew the exact order in which each hut would be visited. Two men from one of the huts that the guards always checked first furtively hurried over to Plüschow's and Trefftz's hut and got into their beds.

Again, in their cramped, damp hiding place, the two escapers listened out for any clue that their escape had been discovered. But the dull routine of Donington Hall went on, as unchanged as ever.

"So far, so good," said Plüschow, "so let's go!"

"For Heaven's sake, don't knock anything over," said Trefftz. "Any noise and we'll have dogs barking and alarm bells ringing, and we'll be finished."

Like dark shadows the two men rose from the tangle of chairs, and made their way to the wire.

"Watch out for the fourth strand up," said Plüschow. "That one is electric. Touch that and it sets off an alarm in the camp."

"How did you know that?" said Trefftz.

"It pays to eavesdrop!" said Plüschow. "I overheard two of the guards talking about it."

Slowly, slowly, one by one, the two men climbed the wire. If they were careful, and they took care to untangle any bit of clothing that had caught on a barb, it was quite easy to get over. But still, Plüschow made a large rip in his trousers when he jumped the final six feet down to the ground.

Away from the wire, in a dense forest that stood by the road away from the camp, they buried their military coats and caps under drifting leaves and brushwood.

"Now, which way to Derby?" said Trefftz.

But even as he spoke, a soldier loomed out of the dark towards them. Plüschow immediately grabbed Trefftz, hugged him tightly and began to kiss him!

Trefftz was too startled to do anything but go along with this ploy. When the soldier walked past them hurriedly, tutting with embarrassment, he had to grit his teeth to stop giggling.

The danger passed and Plüschow released his companion with a smirk.

"Unseemly conduct for an officer and a gentleman," said Trefftz primly.

They hurried down the road, wanting to get as far away from the camp, and anyone who might recognize them, as quickly as possible. An hour or so later, they came to a crossroads.

A sign stood at the corner of the road, but it was so dark they could not see what it said. Plüschow climbed up it and traced the letters with his finger.

"D… E… R… B…"

"Derby. Yes, this is it. Let's go!"

They walked all night, spurred on by the knowledge that as soon as their escape was discovered, the station was the first place the police and army would look.

As dawn broke, they stopped to tidy themselves up. Plüschow repaired his trousers with a needle and thread that he always carried. Then they shaved, using their own spit as shaving foam.

Doing this was faintly repulsive, but anything that gave a policeman or soldier any clue that they might be two runaways, rather than a couple of well-dressed gentlemen, had to be avoided at all costs.

Shortly after, they reached the railway station and bought train tickets to London. Standing on the near-deserted platform with a handful of early morning passengers made Plüschow feel uneasy.

"Look, my friend," he said to Trefftz, "we're too obvious together. Let's split up. I'll see you in London, on the steps of St. Paul's Cathedral, at seven o'clock this evening."

Trefftz thought that was a good idea. He gave his friend a wink, then wandered to the other end of the platform.

The train arrived, the two men got on and Plüschow's journey passed in a sleepy haze. Once in London, he headed for St. Paul's, but Trefftz didn't appear. Plüschow waited an hour, then headed for Hyde Park, where he thought he could hide and sleep.

But the park was closed, and Plüschow crept into the garden of a nearby house, and hid in the bushes. Unlike the night before, this summer evening was dry and warm, and Plüschow began to nod off to sleep. Then a noise disturbed him and he came to his senses with a start.

A party was going on in the house, and some of the guests had come out onto the lawn to enjoy the night air. Plüschow froze, hardly daring to breathe. A few feet away, elegant gentlemen and ladies in long ball gowns swanned around making conversation. Once he had become used to it, Plüschow found it all quite funny, and enjoyed listening to the party guests as they traded scandalous gossip, or complained about their servants.

As he began to relax, the sound of a piano and a woman singing a beautiful song drifted from an open French window. The guests all returned to the party to hear the performance, and Plüschow fell asleep, lulled by the soft music.

Time passed, and footsteps woke him again. This time it was a couple of patrolling policemen on the other side of the wall. Dawn was breaking, and Plüschow decided this garden was not the best place to be lurking. When the coast was clear, he leaped over the wall and headed again for Hyde Park, which opened at dawn.

Here he found a bench to lie on and slept until nine. Then he headed down to nearby South Kensington to buy his breakfast. Taking a bite out of his bacon and egg sandwich, he began to feel that his escape was all going rather well. But then he heard a cry that made his blood turn to ice.

"Read-all-about-it!" yelled a paper boy. "German officers in camp breakout!"

Next to the boy a huge poster carried news of his escape.

Plüschow bought a paper and scuttled onto the Underground to read it. Trefftz had been caught the previous day, so the police were now concentrating all their efforts on finding Plüschow.

The description it gave made him feel even more uncomfortable:

"He is particularly smart and dapper in appearance, has very good teeth, which he shows somewhat prominently when talking or smiling, is very English in manner and knows this country well."

Ordinarily, he would have been pleased by such a description, but this was all too accurate. Knowing he might be recognized at any moment made Plüschow extremely nervous. He would have to change his appearance at once.

The overcoat was the first thing to go. Plüschow was so fond of it he couldn't bear to throw it away. So, rather foolishly, he took it to a cloakroom at Blackfriars Station. When he handed it over, the attendant asked him his name. By now he was badly flustered and fearful of being arrested at any second. Not thinking straight, he replied in German.

"Meinen?" (meaning 'Mine?')

"Oh, I see," said the attendant, mishearing him. "Mr. Mine. M.I.N.E. OK then," and he handed over a receipt.

Two policemen nearby stared over at him, wondering why this fashionable young man was looking so uncomfortable. Plüschow headed for the exit and walked towards the Thames. Wandering along the embankment he took off his hat, collar and tie and dropped them discreetly into the river.

Next, he went into a general store and bought a tube of ointment and a tin of black boot polish, and then visited a hat shop to buy a worker's flat cap. Heading into a quiet alley, he mixed the ointment and boot polish with coal dust he'd found on the street, and worked it carefully into his blond hair. He dirtied his tailored suit and scuffed his shoes, and rubbed more coal dust into his new hat.

Placing the cap on his head, he caught his reflection in a window. Dashing Gunther Plüschow had gone. Before him stood George Mine – a docker in desperate need of a good bath. Plüschow laughed when he saw himself, but still he looked too respectable. He thought he ought to slouch a bit more. He put his hands in his pockets, and spat on the pavement, as he imagined dock workers did. His disguise in place, he ambled back to Hyde Park, trying hard not to turn into the proud, upright military man he naturally was.

Plüschow had plenty of time to find a safe hiding place before the park closed. The next day, while on a bus, he heard two businessmen talking about a boat named the *Mecklenburg*, that sailed from Tilbury Docks, just outside London, to Holland at two every morning. Realizing this was his best route out of England, he immediately took a train down to Tilbury. Sure enough, there she was – a sea-going ferry operating a daily service between London and Holland. Plüschow hid as close to the ship as he dared and waited for nightfall. He tried to sleep to conserve his energy. Getting aboard was not going to be easy.

Around ten that night, Plüschow waded out into

the river, but immediately sank up to his hips in oozing mud. He made a desperate grab for a discarded plank, and saved himself from a horrible drowning death. After struggling out of the mud, he had no energy for another attempt to reach the ship. Plüschow washed his mud-soaked clothes as best he could and sat on the riverbank, shivering in the dark. Very early the next morning, the *Mecklenburg* sailed away without him. Too cold to sleep, Plüschow watched the dark silhouette of the ferry disappear into the distance. He had never felt so miserable in his life.

The next day was scorching hot, and his clothes dried quickly in the morning sun. They smelled terribly musty, and Plüschow felt very pleased with himself and his dirty docker's disguise! He wandered down to the town to buy a hot sausage sandwich and a sweet cup of tea. Sitting in the sun, wolfing down his breakfast, again he felt full of hope. Today, he told himself, was the day he would leave England for good.

That night Plüschow made another attempt to get out to the *Mecklenburg*. On his travels around the riverfront, he'd noticed a small rowing boat with the oars carelessly left inside. When night fell, he sneaked down to the riverbank and pushed the boat into the water. But his troubles were not yet over. Halfway out to the *Mecklenburg*, his little boat had filled up with so much water that it sank. As he floundered in the river, Plüschow mouthed a silent series of bloodcurdling curses. He threw off his jacket and began to swim towards the ship. Luckily, the tide was with him. A less athletic man would have drowned, but all those games of hockey at Donington had kept him fit.

He reached the ferry within ten minutes, and clung to the anchor cable as he got his breath back. Then, summoning his last ounce of strength, he pulled himself up onto the ship. His luck held. No one spotted him coming aboard, so he found himself a lifeboat and hid under the canvas cover. It was a warm night and when the water had dried from his skin he drifted off into a deep, dreamless sleep.

"PEEEEEEEPPPHHH!!!"

Plüschow woke with a start. Was that a police whistle? Had they caught him? Then it came again.

"PEEEEEEEPPPHHH!!!"

No, he realized, it was the ship's horn. He peered out of his canvas cover to see that the *Mecklenburg* was about to dock in the port of Rotterdam in Holland. He'd done it!

Feeling very pleased with himself, Plüschow did something really reckless. He pulled out his knife, sliced open the canvas above his head, and slowly stood up, revealing himself to all around. Much to his surprise, no one took the slightest bit of notice. The crew was busy preparing to dock, and the passengers were rounding up their luggage. This was probably a good thing. Plüschow looked absolutely filthy, which might easily have aroused people's suspicions. Had they not been so preoccupied, he could well have been arrested on the spot and sent back to England.

Realizing he had done something foolish, Plüschow crouched beneath the covers again, and waited until the last few passengers were getting off the boat. He mingled with them, probably mistaken for a particularly dirty member of the ship's crew. Once on the quayside he headed for a door marked 'Exit forbidden', and then he was free.

Strolling into the town, he booked himself into a hotel, had a long bath and ate a meal big enough for three. The next day he caught a train back to Germany. After an extraordinary nine months since his escape from China, Gunther Plüschow was once again ready to fight for his country.

AFTER THE ESCAPE

Plüschow seems rather like a comic book hero from another age, and perhaps it was oddly fitting that in later life he would meet a heroic death.

On his return home from England in 1915, he was awarded the Iron Cross medal for bravery, presented to him personally by the German king, Wilhelm II. He survived the war to write about his adventures in England in the book *My Escape from Donington Hall*, from which much of the information in this story is taken.

After the war he took up another great love – exploration. As a child he had been fascinated by Tierra del Fuego ('The Land of Fire'). Found at the tip of South America, this wild and rugged landscape was one of the last unexplored places on Earth. Plüschow became the first man to fly over this land and continued to explore, photograph and film the territory until January 1931.

That month, he and his co-pilot, Ernest Dreblow, had to make a forced landing with their seaplane, in a desolate lake surrounded by glaciers. The descent badly damaged one of the floats the plane used for its landing gear. In dreadful, freezing conditions, Plüschow and Dreblow battled for three days to fix their float. Eventually they managed to take off, but soon afterwards the aircraft's wing fell off. Plüschow parachuted from the plane, but his chute failed to open and he fell to his death. The plane crashed into another lake. Dreblow wasn't killed in the landing, but froze to death after swimming ashore. Plüschow's flight diary was found with his body and tells of their heroic and tragic misadventure.

CHAPTER FIVE

ESCAPE OR DIE

André Devigny lay on the bed in his small cell at Montluc military prison in Lyon, France. It was August 20th, 1943. He pulled his musty blankets around his head, trying to gain some warmth from the rough, thin material. The light creeping in under his door told him it was morning. Ahead lay another day of questioning and torture, just like every other day for the last two weeks.

As he drifted in and out of sleep, he could hear noises. The prison was waking up. Far away, a door

88

slammed. Guards shouted. Then, closer now, several heavy footsteps and the rattle of keys on a ring. The footsteps stopped outside his door, and the lock was drawn back. As the door opened, bright sunlight spilled in, and Devigny covered his eyes with his hand. Three German guards had come for him. One spoke curtly, in the few words of French he had learned at Montluc.

"Out. Now. Hurry."

But Devigny was not taken away to be tortured. Instead, he was dragged before a senior Nazi officer and told he was to be shot within the next few days. Bundled back to his cell, he was handcuffed and left with his thoughts. He was 26 years old, and a violent death was staring him in the face.

Devigny was not surprised by the news of his execution. He was a member of the French Resistance – a group of men and women who continued to fight against the German soldiers who had invaded their country during the Second World War. Four months before, in April 1943,

Devigny had killed a German spy, and had been arrested several days later.

Montluc was where they took him. This grim, dark prison was a last bleak home to thousands of Resistance fighters, as well as Jewish prisoners who were held here before being transported to special camps to be killed. No prisoner who entered Montluc had ever escaped.

Devigny was tortured by the Nazi secret police, but gave nothing away. Once his captors realized he was not going to talk, it was time to kill him. Devigny wasn't going to go without a fight, but he was weak from his ordeal. How could he break out of such a fortress?

As night fell, Devigny began to plot. A small smile played around his lips. He still had a few tricks up his sleeve, and now was the time to play them. He may have been handcuffed, but his cuffs were not a serious problem. When Devigny arrived at Montluc, a fellow prisoner had slipped him a pin and he had soon learned to pick the lock on the cuffs. His jailers had given him a single metal spoon to eat his meals, and he had scraped the edge of the handle on the cold stone floor until it was as sharp as a chisel. Using this, he had quickly discovered he could remove a couple of slats from the bottom of his wooden cell door. While the guards were not making their rounds, he would squeeze out onto the corridor and talk to his fellow prisoners. He had also had a good look around.

Devigny's cell was on the top floor of the prison block. There was a window at the end of the corridor which led out onto the roof. Between his cell block and the outside of the prison there was a courtyard, another block and an outer wall. It was a lot to get through.

On one of his trips out to the corridor, Devigny had come across a lamp frame, carelessly left by the prison guards. Made up of three metal prongs, it would make a perfect grappling hook, if only he had a rope to attach it to. Devigny didn't have a rope, but he did have a razor blade – a priceless gift slipped to him by another fellow prisoner. He began to shred some of his clothes and blankets into long, thin strips. He bound these together, along with wire from his mattress, to make a rope strong enough to hold his weight.

Devigny worked long into the night, furiously fighting off the desire to sleep. His head nodded down from time to time, but he struggled on. He told himself there would be time enough to rest during the day, when the guards would take far more interest in what he was doing. He made the rope as long as his shredded clothes and blankets would let him, and hid it under his bed. If the guards had bothered to search his cell they would have found the rope easily enough, but they were confident their handcuffed prisoner would be unable to do anything to escape.

Devigny fell asleep around dawn. Some time later his cell door crashed open, and he woke with a start. He imagined this was a squad of soldiers, come to take him to the firing squad. Relief swept through him as he realized that it was only another prisoner being delivered to his cell.

One of the guards jeered: "Hey Devigny, you've got some company in your final hours."

The teenage boy who joined him sat sullenly in the corner. After a while, the two of them fell into guarded conversation, sizing each other up. Bit by bit, the newcomer told him his name was Gimenez, and he too had been arrested for working with the Resistance.

This new arrival was a problem. What if Gimenez was a spy, come to make sure Devigny did not escape? What if he was so desperate to avoid torture or execution, he would betray Devigny in the hope of saving his own life? Even if he was neither of these things, there was a rule at Montluc prison that any prisoner who did not inform the guards that their cellmate was trying to escape would be shot. If Devigny went, Gimenez would have to come too. There was no other way.

Devigny decided he had no choice but to trust this stranger.

"Look," he said to him quietly, "I've had it here. Any day now…"

He drew a finger across his throat.

"I've worked out a way of getting out, and I've got to go really soon. You'll have to come with me too. They'll shoot you if you stay and don't give me away."

Gimenez looked terrified.

"Of course I won't give you away," he said quickly. His voice sounded tearful, and desperate. "But can't you see I'm in enough trouble already?"

Devigny agreed. "But don't think they won't torture you, then kill you," he said, "just because you're young. Come with me. If you stay here, you'll die. If you escape, at least you've got a chance…"

Gimenez sighed a deep, troubled sigh.

"OK," he said softly, and the two prisoners fell silent.

So, on the night of August 24th, 1943, Devigny

and Gimenez began their escape. The first part was easy. After the guards had settled down, the two prisoners squeezed their way through the already loosened wooden slats on the door and out into the corridor. Next came the window. Devigny stood on Gimenez's shoulders and began to force it open. Already he felt weak, and wondered if he had the strength to make such an exhausting escape. But the window gave way to a mild heave, and Devigny hauled himself out onto the roof. Gimenez followed behind.

Standing on the roof, breathing in the cold, fresh air, they both felt an odd sense of freedom. The night was clear, still and moonless – perfect for an escape, with only the prison lights casting a dim glaze over the route before them. But, on a night like this, the slightest sound would carry all too easily, and alert the prison guards. Still, luck was with them again. A railway ran right past the prison, and every ten minutes trains thundered past. Their coming and going would hide the noise the two men might make for a good minute or two.

They crept forward to the edge of the block and looked down onto the courtyard below. By now their eyes had grown used to the dark. They could spot the position of the guards by the occasional glow of a cigarette end, or the glimmer of a belt buckle or bayonet as it caught in a floodlight. Plotting out the route they would have to take, Devigny saw that one guard stood exactly in their path. This man would have to die.

"Look, this is what we'll do," Devigny whispered to Gimenez. "When the time is right I'll climb down and deal with the guard there, while you wait here. When we can get through, I'll whistle once. So listen out!"

Gimenez looked very afraid.

"If we kill a guard, they'll shoot us on the spot!" he said.

He was swallowing hard, his eyes wide with fear. Devigny spoke firmly, and placed a hand on his friend's shoulder.

"We're dead men already, Gimenez, unless we get out of here."

As they stood on the roof, the prison clock struck midnight. While the chimes rang out, one group of guards was replaced by another. Low voices muttered cheerless greetings and the new guards settled down to a long, dull night. Devigny and Gimenez looked down unseen for a whole hour, taking in any routine or change of position the guards might make.

The clock struck one. As the single chime faded into the night, a goods train thundered by. It was time to go. Devigny lowered his rope into the gloom. It was so dark he didn't even know whether it would touch the ground. When there was no more rope to lower, he swung over the edge and slithered down the side of the block. He was so jittery he cut his hand on a piece of wire threaded into the rope. But the rope was long enough to take him to the courtyard. There he waited, hidden by black shadows, until another train passed and he raced over to the other side of the yard. Before him, staring in the opposite direction, stood the guard.

Devigny looked at the man with some pity. There he was, bored, restless, waiting for his shift to end, probably longing for a hot breakfast and a comfy bed. But to escape and save his own life, Devigny would have to kill him in cold blood.

The guard turned to face him and Devigny sprang from the shadows. He grabbed him by the throat, and then killed him with his own bayonet.

The dead man was swiftly hauled into the shadows, his leather boots dragging softly on the floor. Devigny waited to see if their struggle had been overheard, but the night was as still and silent as before. He made a low whistle, and Gimenez hurried over to join him. Their path was clear up to the next block, but Devigny was shaking with exhaustion and fear, and too weak to climb the side of the building.

"You'll have to go first," he whispered to

Gimenez. "I haven't got the strength to climb."

Gimenez climbed up the building. He passed the rope down to Devigny, who had now realized his companion was essential to his escape, rather than the pest he imagined he would be. They hurried across the roof of the block and peered over. They were on the outer edge of the prison. Only a perimeter wall fifteen feet away stood between them and freedom.

But as they crouched on the roof, they heard an odd squeaking sound.

"What the devil is that?" whispered Gimenez.

They found out soon enough. Below, circling around the ground between the prison buildings and the wall, was a guard on a bicycle. He made the trip around the prison boundary every three minutes.

So close to success, Devigny was seized by a desperate need to get the whole escape over with. Their cell lay empty. The skylight to the roof had been opened. Worst of all, a dead man lay in the shadows. Surely, at any moment, a prison guard would find some clue to an escape and raise the alarm? With every passing minute the chance of discovery grew greater. But Devigny kept these thoughts to himself. The last thing he wanted to do was give Gimenez even more cause to panic.

Then, their chances began to look even more desperate.

"Listen," said Devigny, "I can hear voices below. There must be a couple of guards beneath us too."

But when the cyclist rode by, the men could see that he was talking to himself. Both breathed a long sigh of relief and got ready for the final push.

As the clock struck three, Devigny threw the rope over to the outer wall. The lamp frame grapple gripped the brickwork, and held firm. They tied their end of the rope to a solid chimney stack and prepared to cross. But, just at that moment, the guard on the bicycle decided it was time for a rest. He parked his bike right below the men and stood beneath them wheezing.

Devigny and Gimenez couldn't believe how unlucky they were. Agonizing minutes passed, each man expecting to hear the cry of a guard raising the alarm at any second. In the east, a pale light touched the rim of the sky. Soon it would be dawn. But the guard below never did look up to see their rope. He got back on his bike and cycled off.

It was now or never, but the strain was beginning to show all too clearly on the two escapers.

Devigny spoke softly: "You go first, Gimenez, and I'll follow."

"No…" said the boy fiercely. "What if the rope breaks? What if I get spotted and shot? What if I fall? You go and I'll follow."

Devigny's patience was at an end, and he snapped: "Go now, or I'll throttle you on the spot."

A fierce, whispering argument continued between them. Eventually Devigny threw himself onto the rope and hauled himself over as fast as he could. Gimenez followed swiftly after, and the two edged along the outer wall until they came to a place where it was low enough to jump down to the ground.

Dropping with a dull, muffled thump, they were free. The prison had no uniform, so Devigny and Gimenez were able to mingle with workers on their way to the early morning shift at a nearby factory. By the time their empty cell and the dead body of the guard had been discovered, the two prisoners had vanished into the nearby countryside.

AFTER THE ESCAPE

André Devigny escaped to Switzerland, and made his way to North Africa where he joined up with French army forces. After the war, French president General De Gaulle awarded him the Cross of Liberation medal, and gave him an important job in the French secret service. In 1957, French director Robert Bresson made a movie of the escape from Montluc. It was shot at the prison and the actors even used the same rope that Devigny and Gimenez had used. Devigny was hired as an advisor on the movie. He retired in 1971, and died in 1999.

Gimenez, his companion in the escape, was not so lucky. He was recaptured and although his fate is unknown, he was almost certainly executed.

CHAPTER SIX

MUSSOLINI'S MOUNTAINTOP GETAWAY

Nazi dictator Adolf Hitler received the bad news in his secret headquarters – the 'Wolf's Lair' at Rastenburg, hidden away in a dark forest in East Prussia. His friend and Germany's ally Benito Mussolini, fascist dictator of Italy for the last 20 years, had been toppled from power.

The reports that came in were sketchy, but deeply alarming. Mussolini had been popular in Italy, until he had led his country into the Second World War on the side of Nazi Germany. The

Italian people didn't want a war, and many Italian troops didn't want to fight. Then, in the summer of 1943, British, American and other Allied troops invaded the south of Italy and were now working their way up to Rome. Mussolini had been arrested and driven off to a secret location. An Italian general, Marshall Badoglio, was the new leader of Italy.

Hitler was not just worried about his friend. With Mussolini gone, the Italians might make peace with Germany's enemies, or even worse, change sides. There were already hundreds of thousands of German troops in Italy, there to fight side by side with their ally. Now they would have to take over the country, rather than be there as friends. This would not help the Germans at all.

The Nazi leader quickly realized that the way to solve the problem was to find Mussolini and help him escape. Once he was free, the Germans could use their soldiers to make him leader of Italy again. But the Italians knew this too, so they would be hiding Mussolini very carefully. What Hitler needed was a daring rescue mission. An aide told him he had just the man for the job.

On the morning of July 26th, SS-Colonel Otto Skorzeny stood nervously in an outer office of the 'Wolf's Lair'. The first thing anyone noticed about Skorzeny was his huge size. Tall, and built like an ox, he was a menacing figure. The second thing they noticed was the scar on his left cheek. This was the result of a sword fight he'd had when he was a student.

Skorzeny came from a long line of military men, and was a natural daredevil and leader. When the Second World War began, he joined the SS – a branch of the German military made up of the most fanatical Nazi troops. He fought in Eastern Europe and Russia, then took a job training SS commando troops – special units that would carry out unusual and very risky missions. Now he had the chance to show what his men could do.

Hitler greeted Skorzeny with great formality,

and told him he was to fly to Italy at once and rescue his friend. The plan was to be given the codename *Operation Eiche* (Operation Oak).

Skorzeny told Hitler he would free Mussolini or die in the attempt. But, as he walked away, his mind was already racing, wondering how he could carry out what seemed like an impossible task. If he knew where Mussolini was, he could plan the escape. But how could he find that out?

German spies snooped where they could, and German radio operators secretly listened in to all Italian military radio messages, hoping to pick up clues. The situation was difficult. It was true many Italians hated their former leader, especially those who had lost fathers and sons in the war. But there were still many others, especially in the armed forces, who still supported him.

Skorzeny heard Mussolini had been taken to the island of Ponza, near to Rome. Then he was transferred to an Italian naval base at La Maddalena, an island off Sardinia. But he was moved again, and it was several weeks before another clue gave away his location.

Meanwhile, events in Italy had moved on. On September 8th, 1943, Badoglio's government ordered its troops to stop fighting against the British and Americans, and Italy was now no longer at war. German troops in Italy immediately took over important military bases, disarmed Italian troops where they could, and seized Rome. But there was still a grave danger that the Italians would turn against the German soldiers based there.

With all this going on around him, Skorzeny had a change of fortune. He had found out that Mussolini was being held by an Italian General named Gueli. When a coded message from Gueli was intercepted, giving away his hiding place, Skorzeny sprang into action.

Mussolini had been flown to a winter ski resort – the Albergo-Rifugio hotel near Gran Sasso, the highest peak in the Apennine Mountains, eighty miles northeast of Rome. He was being held by 250 Italian troops. It was a well-chosen spot: remote, and accessible to the outside world only by cable car.

Skorzeny considered his options. It was impossible to attack from below, but too dangerous to send in parachute troops, who would be scattered by high winds and dashed to pieces on the mountainside. The only option left was gliders. Gliders were dangerous too. They were flimsy, clumsy things, but they made no noise. The more he thought about it, the better an idea it seemed. In fact, gliders would be perfect. They would land silently next to the hotel, and his men could rush out and seize Mussolini before the Italian soldiers knew what was happening. At least that was what he hoped.

On September 10th, Skorzeny took a flight over the hotel to photograph likely landing spots, and the planning began in earnest. September 12th was chosen as the day of the attack, and an Italian general named Soleti agreed to come along on the mission. A supporter of Mussolini, Skorzeny had brought him along to call out to the Italian troops and order them not to fire.

On the morning of the attack, Skorzeny's SS commandos and a detachment of German *Luftwaffe* parachutists gathered on the runway of an airbase in Rome. As they stood waiting for their gliders to be readied, many ate an early lunch, wondering if this would be the last meal they would ever eat.

But before they could board the gliders, American planes swooped over the airfield, dropping bombs on the runway. The troops scattered. Although no one was hurt, the runway now had several large bomb craters in it.

After a brief inspection Skorzeny decided his planes could still take off, and the attack proceeded as planned. There were twelve gliders, soon packed with Skorzeny's men and their equipment, ready to be towed into the air by powerful German bombers. But as soon as they started to take off, things started to go wrong. Two of the gliders hit bomb craters and crashed during take-off, including the one Skorzeny had ordered to lead the attack. Now he would have to lead the way himself. Inside his cramped glider, he was wedged into his seat by the equipment he carried and couldn't move to see where they were going. So he hacked a hole with a bayonet in the flimsy canvas at the side of the glider, to improve his view.

During the journey, another two gliders became separated from the others in dense cloud and lost their way. Now there were only eight gliders left. After an hour they were near to their target. The tow ropes that held the gliders to the bombers were released, and the bombers flew quickly away so the thunderous sound of their engines wouldn't alert the Italian troops below. The gliders swooped silently down to the hotel like strange sinister birds. But, as they got closer to the landing site Skorzeny had chosen, he realized it was much smaller and more dangerous than he had thought.

It was covered with boulders and sloped steeply down to a deep ravine.

But it was too late to go back now. Skorzeny had promised Hitler he would rescue Mussolini at any cost. So he brusquely ordered his pilot to land. His glider hit the ground and sliced its way through a rock-strewn meadow, but after a very bumpy landing, it came to a halt a mere sixty feet from the hotel.

Expecting to be cut down at any second by a hail of machine-gun fire, Skorzeny and his men quickly poured out of the glider and stormed into the hotel entrance. Amazingly, no shots were fired. Perhaps the Italians had been caught completely by surprise? Or perhaps General Soleti, who was right behind Skorzeny shouting to the Italian troops not to shoot, had persuaded them not to defend the hotel.

Inside the hotel, Skorzeny noticed two Italian officers operating a radio set. He kicked it over, smashing it to pieces, and sprinted up the main staircase. By a stroke of luck, Mussolini was in the first room he entered. Two stunned Italian officers guarding him were quickly overpowered. Now that he had the Italian leader with him, Skorzeny called upon the Italian troops to surrender.

There was a short pause before the Italian commanding officer accepted defeat. A white sheet was hung from a hotel window, and an Italian colonel presented Skorzeny with a goblet of red wine. Amazingly, not a shot had been fired in the attack, which had lasted a mere four minutes. As the Italians surrendered, the last of the gliders were landing outside the hotel. The only dead and injured in this extraordinary mission were the German troops in crashed gliders.

Mussolini was now in German hands, but Skorzeny still had to get him away before the alarm was raised and more Italian troops arrived to stop them. This could prove to be just as dangerous as the initial attack. He had originally intended to take the Italian leader off the mountain by the cable car next to the hotel, but now he realized the best way out was to fly. Overhead circled a small *Storch* reconnaissance plane, which had been sent to overlook the mission from the air. This spindly two-seater plane could land and take off in a tiny space. If anything was going to get Mussolini off the mountain it was this.

Skorzeny radioed orders for the pilot to land, while his soldiers frantically cleared away boulders, stones and parts of broken glider from the meadow, to make the landing spot safer. The *Storch* came to a stop right in front of them. Mussolini squeezed in next to the pilot, while Skorzeny eased himself in behind him. The pilot protested strongly that the plane wasn't meant for three. But Skorzeny felt personally responsible for Mussolini's safety, and wasn't going to let him out of his sight until they'd both returned to Germany.

But the *Storch* was perilously overloaded. The pilot revved the engine to maximum power, with his brakes on and Skorzeny's soldiers holding onto the plane to keep it steady. Then the brakes came off, the soldiers let go, and the *Storch* bumped across the meadow trying to build up speed. Before it was properly airborne, it lurched over the edge of the mountainside and plummeted to the valley below. The ground loomed alarmingly. But the pilot was highly skilled and, as the plane picked up speed, he eased it out of its near-fatal dive and climbed above the mountains, heading for Rome.

Crammed into the small cockpit, Skorzeny spent an uncomfortable flight straining to hear the Italian dictator over the noise of the aircraft engine, as he raged against his captors. Only when the *Storch*'s wheels hit the runway of the German airforce base in Rome, did Skorzeny finally relax. He had promised Hitler he would rescue his friend. Now here he was, sitting next to the Italian dictator, safe in German hands, with both of them alive to tell the tale.

AFTER THE ESCAPE

Once they had reached Rome, Mussolini and Skorzeny flew to Hitler's 'Wolf's Lair' headquarters in East Prussia. Hitler was overjoyed to see his friend again. He put Mussolini back in charge of the part of Italy still occupied by Nazi Germany, and fighting there went on until the end of the war. However, in the spring of 1945, Mussolini was finally captured by Italian rebels and executed in the street.

CHAPTER SEVEN

OVER THE WALL WITH A LUMINOUS HAMMER

Heinz Holzapfel stared from an upper window
of the 'House of Ministries' in East Berlin where
he worked from time to time as an economist and
spokesman for the East German government.
It was a dreary afternoon in 1965 and East Berlin
was then a shabby, dreary city.

The damage inflicted on it at the end of the
Second World War, twenty years before, had barely
been repaired. Bullet holes and shell blasts still
blighted the walls of many buildings. Bomb sites
and Russian soldiers, who had occupied the city

117

in 1945, were still a very visible part of life. An air of weary despair hung over the streets.

Holzapfel had an unusual view. The office he worked in had an unrestricted outlook over wasteland into West Berlin. The streets there looked clean, and brightly-lit shop signs and window displays livened up the drizzly day. Cars buzzed along busy streets. Cars, Holzapfel couldn't help noticing, produced in all manner of vibrant, cheerful hues. In East Germany the cars were a dull blue or green.

In a normal city Holzapfel could have walked over to those streets in a couple of minutes. But Berlin was not a normal city. The east and west sides were separated by a high wall. In the East, armed guards in watchtowers surveyed the wall, and barbed wire, landmines and fierce guard dogs, acted as a further incentive to not even attempt to cross over.

Not for the first time, Holzapfel reflected that 1932 had not been a good year to have been born in Germany. In his 33 years, he had seen many terrible things. He had survived Hitler and the Nazis, and the horrors of the Second World War. Then, in 1945, his country had been taken over by combined allied forces: the Russians along with the United States, Britain and France. Germany was split in two, with its capital, Berlin, divided between East and West.

In the East, where he lived, the Russians had set up a communist government, which closely controlled all aspects of people's lives. This style of rule was so unpopular that a quarter of East Germans fled to the West, where life was more comfortable and people had greater freedoms. To stop more of them from leaving, the East German government had built this wall. If you were caught trying to cross it, you faced arrest and a long period of imprisonment. That was if you were lucky. If you weren't, you could be killed. Border guards were encouraged with offers of cash rewards, extra days off and promotion, to shoot anyone attempting to escape. But some people still managed to get across and Holzapfel hoped to be one of them. More than that, he intended to bring his wife Jutta, and their nine year old son Günter, with him.

They were here with him now, on this July evening, hiding in this office. When everyone went home, Holzapfel intended to carry out the daring escape that he'd been planning for the last eighteen months. All they had to do was wait until the late evening and then try their luck.

The wall by the House of Ministries was unusual in that it was only 25 feet away from that office block. In most parts of the city there was a clear stretch of closely-guarded open ground around the wall, where escape was next to impossible. But Holzapfel had realized that if he went out onto the roof here, he could throw a rope down right onto the other side, and he and his family might be able to slide down it. It was going to be more complicated than that of course, but Holzapfel was a resourceful man.

Although East Berliners were not allowed to visit West Berlin, this didn't work the other way around. On the western side, family members and friends lined up every day at the checkpoints that controlled access between the two sides of the city, and the Holzapfels were sometimes visited by friends from the West. As Heinz Holzapfel stared out of the window, he hoped his friends would be out there soon, on the other side of the wall as they had promised, ready to help with his escape.

Evening fell and the building slowly emptied. The office clock ticked with intolerable slowness towards the late evening hours. At nine o'clock, the Holzapfels crept carefully out of their hiding place and up marble stairs to the roof, conscious of the fact that the slightest noise could alert the night watchmen who were now the building's sole other occupants.

Up on the roof it was raining hard and they all shivered in what had turned out to be an unusually cold summer evening. But hidden in a corner of the roof were several items that Holzapfel had brought with him on previous occasions and assembled there to help him with his escape. There was a hammer painted in a luminous yellow, and a strange pulley contraption made out of a harness and part of a bicycle wheel.

Five floors below them they could see the wall, brightly lit by arc lights. Anyone trying to get across would find themselves in the gun sights of the border guards within seconds. But shortly before midnight that night, something unusual happened. That section of the wall was suddenly plunged into darkness. The Holzapfels felt a great wave of relief. Their friends in the West were waiting for them and step one of their plan – to cut off the electric power to the wall lights – had been successfully completed.

Heinz Holzapfel went at once to pick up his luminous hammer, and wrapped a cloth around its heavy metal head. Making sure a strong nylon cord was still carefully attached to it, he swung it around and let it fly off into the dark. It landed with a dull 'thunk' on the far side of the wall. Moments later, dark shadows emerged from the shrubs in the wasteland there. The luminous hammer glowed dully on the ground and was easily found. Holzapfel's friends attached a strong wire cable to the nylon thread, which was carefully winched back up to the roof, where it was wrapped around a sturdy metal pipe.

Holzapfel listened carefully over the noise of the late evening traffic, straining to hear if any evidence of their escape had been detected. So far no one had been able to repair the electrical cables that fed the arc lights. He hoped the authorities would think this was just an everyday electric failure, rather than anything more suspicious. With a bit of luck they wouldn't send out an electrician to fix the power supply until the following morning. If they fixed it as a matter of urgency, the escape would be doomed.

On the western side, the cable was anchored

firmly to a truck which had been abandoned there. Everything was in place for the escape to begin.

Günter went first. Carefully strapping him into the harness and hauling him gingerly over the side of the high office roof, Heinz and Jutta Holzapfel kissed their nine-year-old boy and let him slide off into the void. The cable held, the noise of the whizzing bike wheel was not too loud, and a few minutes later they had managed to pull the harness back up to the roof, using the nylon thread that had been originally attached to the hammer.

Jutta went next. The cable sagged under her heavier weight and Heinz watched anxiously, fearing his contraption might not hold up. A fall from this height would kill his wife and almost certainly alert the guards or watchmen in the building. But Jutta slipped safely away and eventually he was able to winch the harness back again.

The escape had been going on for at least half an hour now, and the lights had still not come back on. As Heinz fastened the harness and prepared to leave his old life behind, he wondered how much longer his luck would hold. He too would fall if the cable snapped or slipped, and he too could, even now, be in the sights of border guards who would shoot to kill any escaper without warning, as they had been ordered to do.

As Heinz sat on the parapet, gathering up his courage to make that final leap into the West, he was indeed being observed by soldiers. These weren't East German border guards, but a detachment of Russian soldiers who had a good view of the House of Ministries from their own rooftop observation post. The soldier who had spotted the Holzapfels as they went about their escape summoned an officer. He watched the boy and the woman go down the cable, and then saw Heinz preparing to go.

"Shall I shoot him, comrade officer," said the soldier.

The officer was initially uncertain. "No," he finally decided. "These must be secret agents being smuggled into the West to spy for us. That must be why the lights have been turned off."

So they watched Holzapfel disappear into the dark. Shortly afterwards in the western wasteland, car headlights came on, and engines started. Whatever was going on there had come to an end. The officer and his men shrugged their shoulders and resumed their dreary nocturnal observations.

Heinz Holzapfel's short journey over was not without incident. As he swung and juddered down the cable, important documents, which he was carrying in his pockets, fell out onto the eastern side of the Wall. When he arrived at the end of the cable, he discovered his wife had been injured when she hit the ground. His son, however, was safe and unharmed. Their friends sped them away to a nearby hospital. Once his wife had been treated for her bruises, the family could look forward to making contact with Heinz's three other brothers, all of whom had fled to West Germany before the Wall had been built.

On the eastern side, only daylight revealed the cable still attached from the roof to the truck on the western side. Heinz Holzapfel's dropped documents quickly identified him as the culprit. It's not known what happened to the Soviet soldiers who observed the escape and did nothing to stop it.

The news went unreported in East Germany's newspapers. Elsewhere, the Holzapfels' escape made headlines all over the world.

AFTER THE ESCAPE

Heinz Holzapfel and his family settled into life in West Germany and vanished from history; unlike the Wall, which became a potent symbol of the failure of communism as a political system. People still tried to escape and sometimes they succeeded. More often than not they were arrested or shot and killed. Altogether at least 172 people are known to have been killed trying to get across, and over 60,000 people were sent to prison as a punishment for trying to escape.

As the years went by, the Wall was knocked down and rebuilt, making it even more difficult to breach. From the late 1960s onwards, the best way to get out of East Germany was to pay professional people-smugglers to sneak you out.

The Berlin Wall finally came down in 1989. A year later East and West Germany were reunited into a single nation, and people were once more able to move freely between both sides of Berlin and both sides of the country.